Dear Parent:
Your child's love of reading starts here!

Every child learns to read in a different way and at his or her own speed. You can help your young reader improve and become more confident by encouraging his or her own interests and abilities. You can also guide your child's spiritual development by reading stories with biblical values and Bible stories, like I Can Read! books published by Zonderkidz. From books your child reads with you to the first books he or she reads alone, there are I Can Read! books for every stage of reading:

SHARED READING
Basic language, word repetition, and whimsical illustrations, ideal for sharing with your emergent reader.

BEGINNING READING
Short sentences, familiar words, and simple concepts for children eager to read on their own.

READING WITH HELP
Engaging stories, longer sentences, and language play for developing readers.

READING ALONE
Complex plots, challenging vocabulary, and high-interest topics for the independent reader.

ADVANCED READING
Short paragraphs, chapters, and exciting themes for the perfect bridge to chapter books.

I Can Read! books have introduced children to the joy of reading since 1957. Featuring award-winning authors and illustrators and a fabulous cast of beloved characters, I Can Read! books set the standard for beginning readers.

A lifetime of discovery begins with the magical words "I Can Read!"

Visit www.icanread.com for information on enriching your child's reading experience.
Visit www.zonderkidz.com for more Zonderkidz I Can Read! titles.

Don't be proud at all. Be completely gentle. Be
patient. Put up with one another in love.
— Ephesians 4:2

ZONDERKIDZ

What's Up with Lyle?
Copyright© 2011 Big Idea Entertainment, LLC. VEGGIETALES®, character names,
likenesses and other indicia are trademarks of and copyrighted by Big Idea
Entertainment, LLC. All rights reserved.
Illustrations © 2011 by Big Idea Entertainment, LLC.

Requests for information should be addressed to:

Zondervan, *Grand Rapids, Michigan 49530*

Library of Congress Cataloging-in-Publication Data
Poth, Karen
    What's up with Lyle? / written by Karen Poth.
        p. cm.
    Based on the VeggieTales video: Lyle the kindly Viking.
    ISBN 978-0-310-72160-4 (softcover)
    1. Vikings—Juvenile fiction. I. Big Idea's VeggieTales. II. Title. III. Title: What is
up with Lyle?
    PZ7.P83975Wg 2011
    [E]—dc22.   2010028328

Editor: Mary Hassinger
Art direction: Karen Poth
Cover design: Karen Poth
Interior design: Ron Eddy

Printed in China

10 11 12 13 14 15 16 /SCC/ 21 20 19 18 17 16 15 14 13 12 11 10 9 8 7 6 5 4 3 2 1

ZONDERkidz

I Can Read!™

BEGINNING 1 READING

What's Up with Lyle?

story by Karen Poth

A long time ago,

in a faraway place,

there lived a group of Vikings.

Do you know who the
Vikings were?

Vikings were sailors.

They rode in big ships.

Vikings ate funny food.

They wore furry hats.

Some hats had two horns.

Some hats had one horn.

Some hats had no horns at all!

Most Vikings were mean!
Everyone was scared of
the Vikings.

They were always frowning.

They picked fights with

other Vikings.

They NEVER made their beds.

But this group of Vikings
was not like all the others.
They lived on Noble Island.
They were very nice.

These Vikings NEVER frowned.

They sang a lot of funny songs.

They ALWAYS made their beds.

One day, mean Vikings

came to Noble Island.

"Come with us," Ugalee yelled.

"We are going to rob the monks!"

"We can't come today,"

Sven said.

"We are going to the fair!"

"The fair?" Ugalee laughed.

"You are a Viking!

Vikings do not go to the fair!"

Ugalee was mad at the nice Vikings.

"I will teach them a lesson,"

he said.

Ugalee left Noble Island.

As soon as Ugalee was gone,
Lyle, a young Viking from
the village, stopped by.

"Hi, guys," Lyle said.

"Where are you going?"

"We are going to the fair," Sven said.

"Would you like to come along?"

"Sure!" Lyle answered.

"I will bring my knitting."

Lyle was not like the rest

of the Vikings.

He did not really like

to sail or fish.

Lyle liked to knit.

The Vikings laughed at Lyle.

That hurt his feelings.

On the way to the fair,

Lyle sat by himself on the ship.

The nice Vikings WERE NOT
being nice at all!

But when they reached the fair

all the Vikings had a lot of fun.

Even Lyle!

They played Viking games.

They ate Viking food.

They even swam in the

Viking pool!

Until …

It started to rain.

"Get to the ship!"

the captain yelled.

A huge storm was coming.

The Vikings had to get home.

Sven and his friends ran to the ship.

But there was a BIG problem.

Ugalee and his crew were there.

They had torn the sails.

They had broken the oars.

"We will never get home!"

Ottar cried.

"The sails won't work with holes!

And we cannot row with

broken oars."

"Do not worry," Lyle smiled.

"I know a way!"

He quickly got to work

knitting patches for the sails.

In no time at all

Lyle had fixed the sails.

Lyle saved the day!

The ship sailed back to

Noble Island.

"I'm sorry, Lyle," Sven said.

"We were mean because

you are different."

"And if you weren't different,
we would not have gotten home,"
the captain said.

"Three cheers for Lyle!"

Don't be proud at all. Be
completely gentle. Be patient.
Put up with one another in love.
— Ephesians 4:2